FABLE

The Lion
and the Rat

A FABLE BY

LA FONTAINE

The
Lion and the Rat

Illustrated by

BRIAN WILDSMITH

OXFORD
UNIVERSITY PRESS

One day, a rat

walked, by accident, between a lion's paws.

But the lion
allowed him to
escape, unharmed.

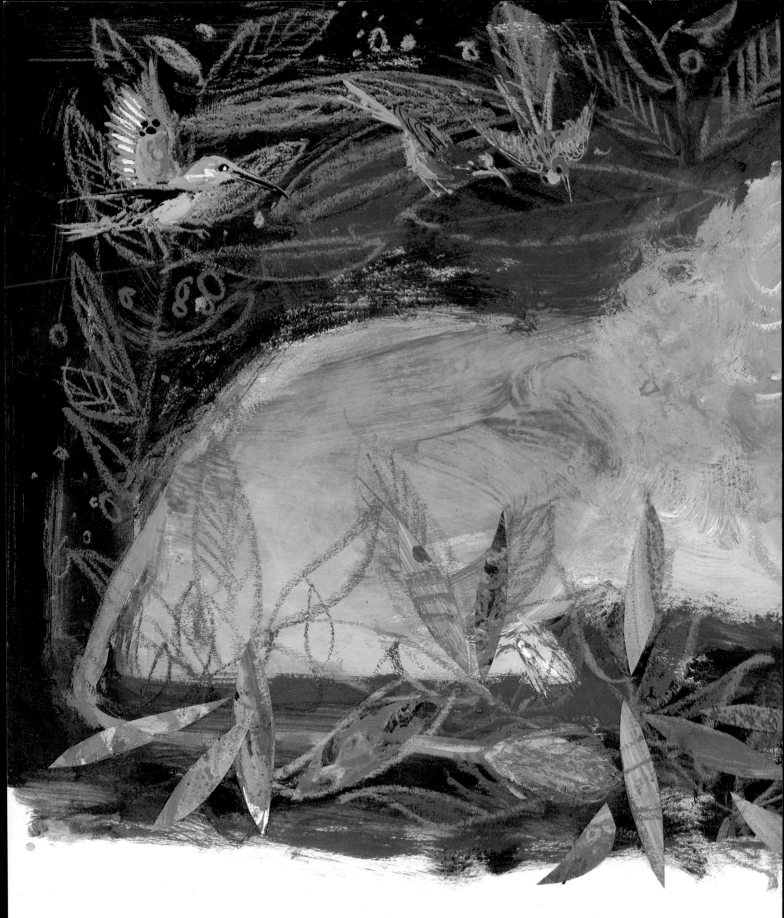

The rat thanked the lion, and said: 'One day
I shall repay you for your kindness.'

The lion laughed to himself.
'How could such a tiny creature
help me, the Lord of the Jungle?'
he thought.

A few months later, the lion was out hunting in the forest when he fell into a trap.

He roared
in fury, and
struggled
with all
his might.

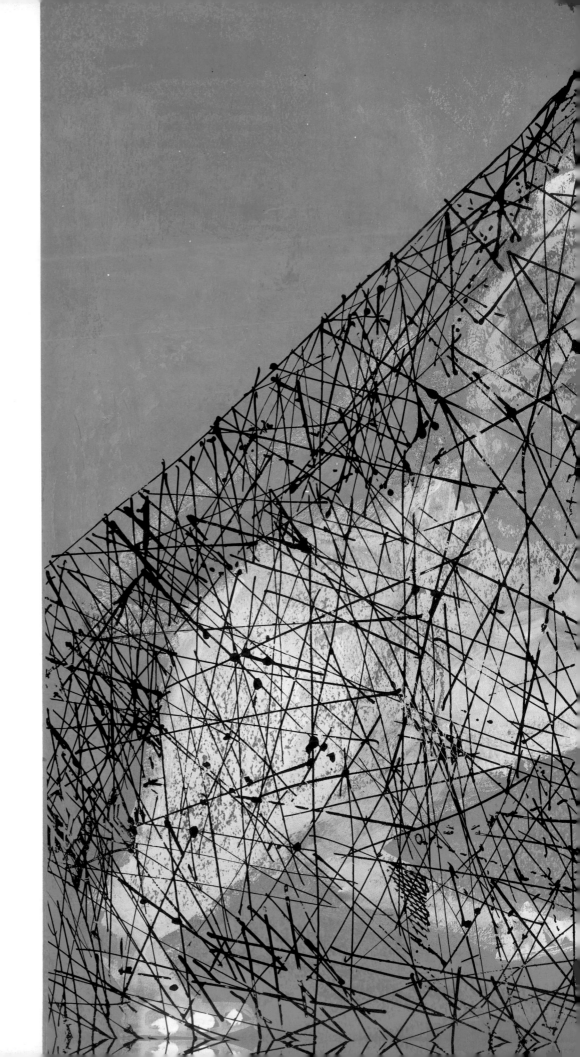

but he could not escape.

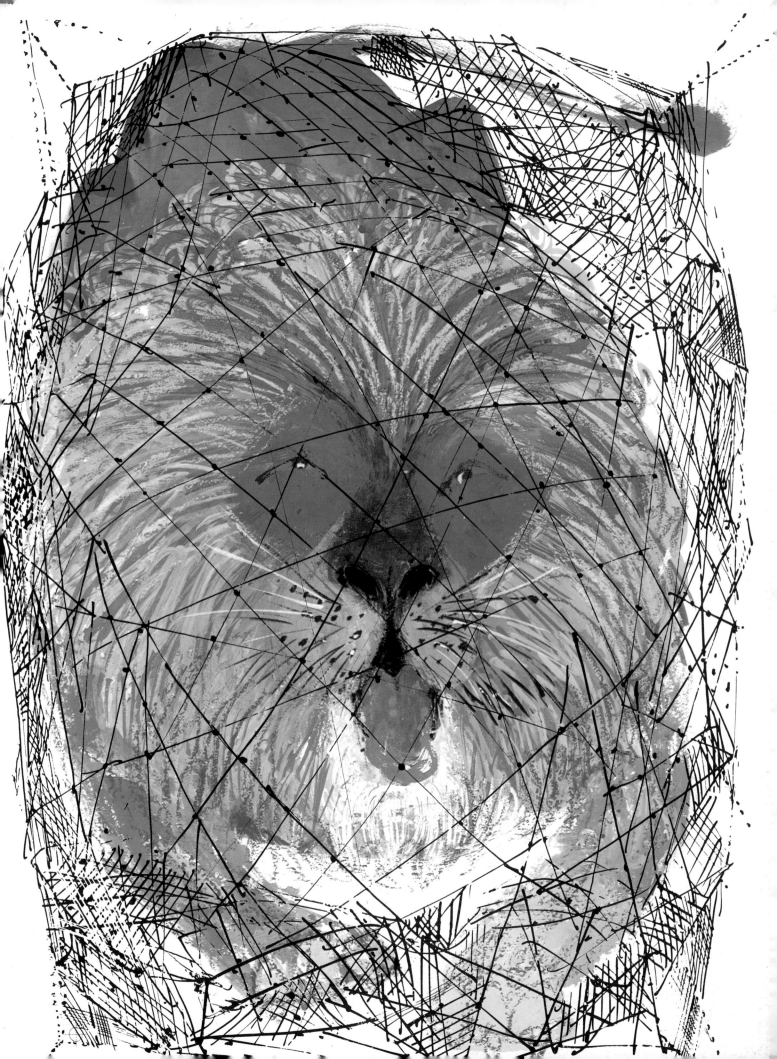

All the animals heard the lion,

and rushed to find him.

The lion asked each of them

in turn for help, but they said: 'How can weak creatures like us help you, the Lord of the Jungle?'

And so they went away.

Just then, the rat came by.
He saw the lion in trouble and ran to help him.

He gnawed and gnawed
right through the net, until
at last the lion was freed.

So the little rat, by patience
and hard work, was able to
do what the lion, in all his
strength and rage, could not.

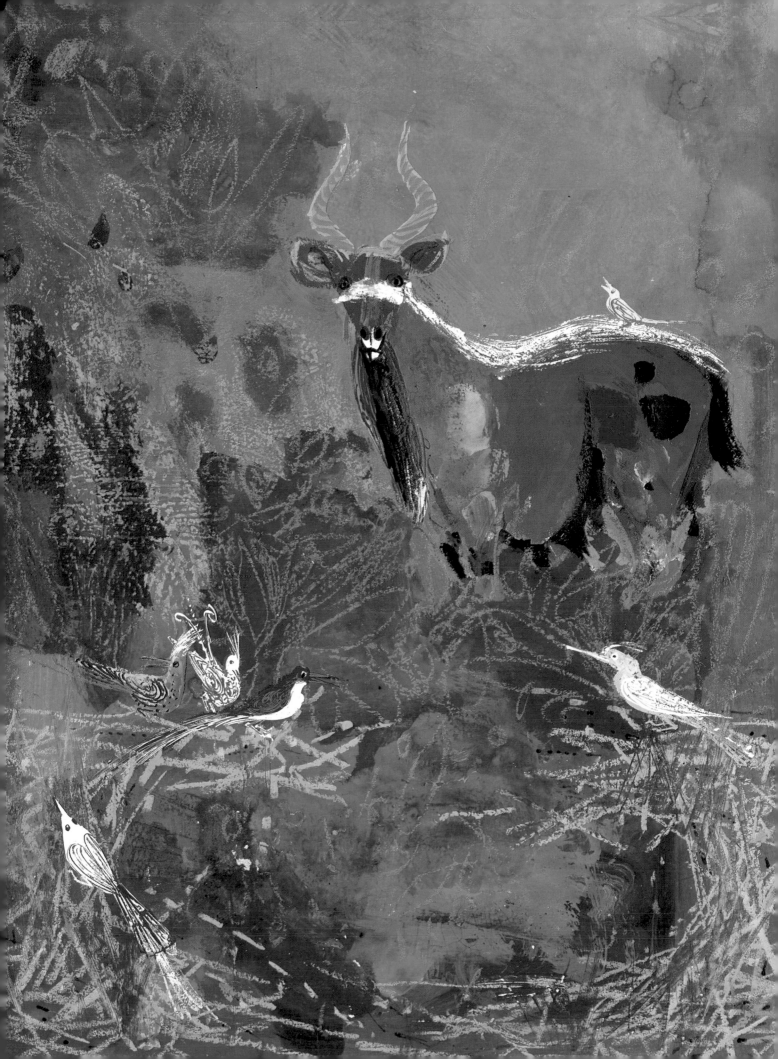

OXFORD

UNIVERSITY PRESS

Great Clarendon Street, Oxford OX2 6DP

Oxford University Press is a department of the University of Oxford.
It furthers the University's objective of excellence in research, scholarship,
and education by publishing worldwide in

Oxford New York

Auckland Bangkok Buenos Aires Cape Town Chennai
Dar es Salaam Delhi Hong Kong Istanbul Karachi Kolkata
Kuala Lumpur Madrid Melbourne Mexico City Mumbai Nairobi
São Paulo Shanghai Singapore Taipei Tokyo Toronto

with an associated company in Berlin

Oxford is a registered trade mark of Oxford University Press
in the UK and in certain other countries